T0198750

MEATBALLS FOR DINNER

Marie Elizabeth Randall Chandler

Meatballs for Dinner

iUniverse books may be ordered through booksellers or by contacting:

iUniverse
1663 Liberty Drive
Bloomington, IN 47403
www.iuniverse.com
1-800-Authors (1-800-288-4677)

Because of the dynamic nature of the Internet, any web addresses or links contained
in this book may have changed since publication and may no longer be valid. The views
expressed in this work are solely those of the author and do not necessarily reflect the
views of the publisher, and the publisher hereby disclaims any responsibility for them.

ISBN: 978-1-5320-9490-3 (sc)
ISBN: 978-1-5320-9491-0 (e)
ISBN: 978-1-5320-9999-1 (hc)

Library of Congress Control Number: 2020913312

Print information available on the last page.

iUniverse rev. date: 07/25/2020

For my sons, Austin and Marshall,
and my granddaughters, Isabella and Gabriella

Meatballs for dinner, they're a strange thing.
Peculiar events they always bring.
Listen now as I tell the story.

It started one day – my son hurried out from school.
His face filled with fear.
I knelt down beside, saying,
"What's wrong, dear?"
"There's an eraser in my ear," he said with a tear.

"Oh my, oh dear, is it so?
It's too deep, I fear!
To the doctor we must go."
"There it is!" I said with a shout as the doctor pulled it out.
"That doctor, he's a winner."

Now on our way to play, and by the way,
"We're having meatballs for dinner!"

There is more in store, do sit as I tell more.

Next came Father, each time he chewed what pain it sent.
So to the doctor he went.

"A big wax ball, surely the cause,"
the doctor said with a shout.
"Oh my, oh dear," cheering in loud applause,
"I'm happy it's out!"

"That doctor, he's a winner! And by the way,
we're having meatballs for dinner!"

Now for the most peculiar event of all, listen as I recall.

It happened one day I was taking a walk.
Father was coming down for a talk.
Along we walked past a big bushy tree,
soon seeing a bug flying straight at me.

Into my ear it went, so deep inside my head.
What a fear it sent, this buzzing I dread.

With a quick shake, I hoped to the air it would take.
But only deeper did it buzz!

"Please, oh please, help me, dear!
There's a bug in my ear!"
"I cannot see any bug," he said with a shrug.

"But it's there!" I wailed, and up the hill I sailed!

"Help! Help!" I cried.
My arms were swinging.
My head was shaking.
My voice was screaming,
"What a horrible feeling this bug is bringing!"

I tore open the door, to the bathroom I ran.
"Help! Help! This bug is alive!
Surely it mustn't survive!"

"Flush it with water!
Water, water, hurry pour!
I don't want to hear it anymore!"

"Could it be? I think it is dead.
There is no buzzing in my head."

Now into the shower I stepped.

No longer I wept.

I washed my hair, still thinking, the bug – is it there?

Yet I must walk, for I must get thinner, and by the way,
"We're having meatballs for dinner!"

The End

A true story!

About the Author

Marie resides in Texas with her husband and seven cats.
She likes to run every day for exercise and
eats healthy organic whole foods.
Her favorite book to read is the Holy Bible.
She reads it every day.
She honors the Lord God in all she does.
Her gift of writing comes from Him.
Meatballs for Dinner is her first children's book.

Printed in the United States
By Bookmasters